SIULUK
THE LAST TUNIQ

Published by Inhabit Media Inc. • www.inhabitmedia.com
Inhabit Media Inc. (Iqaluit), P.O. Box 11125, Iqaluit, Nunavut, X0A 1H0
(Toronto), 191 Eglinton Avenue East, Suite 301, Toronto, Ontario, M4P 1K1

Editors: Neil Christopher and Kelly Ward
Art director: Danny Christopher
Designer: Astrid Arijanto

We acknowledge the support of the Canada Council for the Arts for our publishing
program.

This project was made possible in part by the Government of Canada.

ISBN: 978-1-77227-178-2

Library and Archives Canada Cataloguing in Publication

Sammurtok, Nadia, author
      Siuluk : the last Tuniq / by Nadia Sammurtok ; illustrated by Rob Nix.

ISBN 978-1-77227-178-2 (softcover)

      I. Nix, Rob, illustrator II. Title.

PS8637.A5384S58 2018   jC813'.6   C2017-907608-6

Printed in Canada

SIULUK
THE LAST TUNIQ

BY **NADIA SAMMURTOK**

ILLUSTRATED BY **ROB NIX**

The Tuniit were said to have been giants who lived in the North. They were very strong and could lift rocks no regular man could lift. The Tuniit were also said to be friendly, so they were often referred to as friendly giants.

Siuluk was a strong man. He was often told that he was the last tuniq man alive. Siuluk didn't know whether this was true or not. What he did know was that he was indeed as strong as people said he was, and he remembered his father being a very big, strong man himself.

Siuluk lived alone, not far from a village where Inuit families lived. The Inuit often wondered about Siuluk because he was such a quiet man. Although he was friendly, Siuluk kept to himself and preferred to live alone.

One day, Siuluk was walking home, carrying a walrus over his shoulder after a day of hunting. Along the way, he met up with a group of men from the nearby village. He placed his catch on the ground and greeted them politely.

But these men were not very polite. They asked Siuluk questions about his strength, his size, and about why he spent so much time alone. Since Siuluk was such a gentle man, unkind people from the village would often tease him.

The men asked Siuluk if he had any friends, if he had family, and if it was true that he indeed was as strong as people said he was. The men also questioned Siuluk as to whether he was really the last tuniq man alive.

"So you think you're the last of the friendly giants, strong man?" one of the men teased.

Siuluk did not like their questions.

The men continued to mock Siuluk. They said mean things about his size.

"Siuluk, are you really as strong as people think you are?" one man teased.

"I don't think he is very strong at all," another chimed in.

The men were not friendly to Siuluk, and this upset him. So, he decided to prove his strength to the men.

Siuluk led them to a very large sheet of rock. It was enormous and looked as if it weighed at least a ton. The men quivered at the sight of it.

Siuluk told each man to lift the rock. Hesitantly, each man attempted to lift the rock. But none was successful at even budging the rock from its resting place.

Soon it was Siuluk's turn to try. He squeezed his enormous hands underneath the rock, and with great strength, he lifted it. He bolted it upright. The men watched, stunned at his strength, whispering to one another, "He really is a tuniq!" "How could we have been so foolish as to make fun of a man such as Siuluk?"

Once he returned the rock to its resting place, Siuluk chiselled a challenge on the top of it to anyone who felt the need to prove their strength.

He wrote, "If you are as strong as I am, move this rock."

The men left, humbled and embarrassed. They never bothered Siuluk again.

The men who had challenged Siuluk lived the rest of their lives with the memory of Siuluk, the man who had proven his strength. Every time they passed the rock, they felt humbled and embarrassed about how they had treated Siuluk. They told the story to their children and their children's children, and so the story was passed down from generation to generation, and Siuluk, the last tuniq, was remembered for his strength.

In the hundred years since Siuluk proved his strength, no one has been able to move that rock.

NADIA SAMMURTOK is an Inuit writer and educator originally from Rankin Inlet, Nunavut. Nadia is passionate about preserving the traditional Inuit lifestyle and Inuktitut language so that they may be enjoyed by future generations. Nadia currently lives in Iqaluit, Nunavut, with her family.

AFTERWORD

This is a story I first heard from my father (pictured on the right), who first heard it from his father when he was a child in the earlier part of the 20th century. The story of Siuluk talks about a man who is said to have been one of the last Tuniit to have lived, a man who allegedly lived close by what is now the community of Chesterfield Inlet in Nunavut, Canada, the oldest community in Nunavut. It is a story that has been passed down from generation to generation and is thought to be based on true experiences, with evidence existing of the incident featured in the story. It is a story that intrigued me right when I first heard it from my father. This is a story that focuses on accepting others despite their differences.

—Nadia Sammurtok

Tom Sammurtok, the author's father, in front of Siuluk's rock, 2014